TRAITOROUS TRADERS

Rumors Of Water

Charles Rhodes Jamison

ISBN-978-0-9997108-4-5

Dedicated to farmers and musicians
without which Life has no fruit, herb or spice.

Six months and still no rain. The pond of Rosa has been reduced to a cesspool. A once sparkling body of water now a puddle of scum. When we first arrived villagers scared off ducks, geese too. No ordinary ducks here, the cloistered location gave birth to a new species; some swear they can be spotted at dawn on the horizon - and those lucky enough to have seen the mythical blue duck were possessed by a look of amazement. But that was long ago, the second all of us excitedly arrived the blue ducks booked it! In the distance the blue turned to green and so the myth grew.

Geese ate fish, oh the fish are all dead presently; withal only months ago this scene was different, sure most animals surrounding the pond were scared off - but the geese held their ground. Big gray and white geese that when provoked stood tall, they would spread flight feathers outwards while emitting a loud screeching sound. If that did not deter the menace than the whole flock would stand beside one another. Again that scenery was long ago because the rain hasn't come in months while everybody rinses filthy rags of clothing continuously and worst of all the geese were hunted to extinction - so now we are all starving and dehydrating alongside this stinking puddle of scum.

The filthy stench hole slowly effervescing methane makes anyone nearby noxious. All the trees (what's left) have changed, the perennial leaves started falling weeks ago. Not a tree in sight has leaves. Rumors began spreading that the trees drank from the pond of Rosa by way of roots tapping underground. Even if the rain did arrive, it would have to be a monsoon to sluice away our devastation. You can tell the affect clearly on everybody's face.

When we first got here there was splashing making smiles, us running and playing for miles. We currently fasting all the while, moans and groans make up the sounds. By taking a look around those with some life force seem to be angry and jealous. Nobody does anything constructive! They all wake up and glare at that unholy horizon! Everyday same thing, what's Shelly and Preston up to? Some assume they have fresh water and the most troublesome curiosity of all - where are they going? Where have they been?

See, about three months ago Shelly, Preston and that little brown perky child slipped onto their vessel without saying a word. And so they sit out on the horizon, most people grew mad, fights broke out; groups teamed up to chop down trees making floats but powerful currents swept all endeavors away. The last group paddled vigorously but for every stroke, the float went in opposite direction and honestly was quite funny.

The day was clear and spirits were high, water and crops were still aplenty as with energy but on that day we all laughed at those young boys doing all they could to find out for themselves and all of us - what in God's name are Shelly and Preston up to? Hilarity struck us when those energetic teenagers were making absolutely no head way just some twenty yards off shore.

Poor souls, our mood swapped and nervousness struck once we could no longer see their faces on the crappy float. At close range, they appeared happy, after all they were doing something with their lives. The laughter stopped and then the shouting from shore erupted. We never got to tell those boys how proud all of us were at that moment when they mustered the courage and channeled the dark jealousy for goodness sake.

Silence afterwards. Seems we are all stuck in gloomy sadness, imagining the horror of the deep blue sea's isolation and relentless rays of the sun. A few days have passed but the mood remains - oh those poor boys. Some cling to hope muttering under breath,

"I bet they found new land, I'm sure they will be okay."

To be honest, who knows they could be better off anyway - the air here stinks and the once life saving water hole has become a serious killer. The last person that gave into thirsty temptation died of cholera - oh that sick lady! Gross! Her sounds of pain before death continues to echo in everybody's minds. Some of the more insensitive coined a nickname for that woman, who during the peak of civilization baked the bread from hand picked grain.

Then, like a bad habit the villagers dropped fondness because she fell so ill. One sip, we all saw the action. Had she lived for another day, bet that woman would be leader of the pack. Not being the case, she became tired, sick and so foul smelling the most insensitive carried "sicko" out to the ulterior never to be seen again but heard till this morning.

The real problem...that bright star above shows up everyday without a cloud in its way, okay. One hundred degrees in the shade. Those capable of suffering lick dew off trunks in the morning. When food and water was abundant, we made up stories and fantasies. The only fantasy now preys on the score living...cold water. Fresh, cool spring water, or a mist from the sky.

Perhaps our actions have cursed us. After all, someone mentioned something about digging a crook for a wash puddle designed to flow out to sea if need be. We should have listened to Shelly Jibson. Shelly dug but nobody helped. Shelly asked nicely too, her words clear as the daytime, "Come! Here, wash your rags and clothing so not to pollute." They snickered and ignored,

what's freedom with a boss? And so the story goes, foulness grew in the pond. When the place began to stink and a film materialized on the surface; Shelly shouted one day loudly, "Stop!

All of us must dig channels for the pond to breathe and replenish." Some laughed, most smirked combining a dubious stare but the joke's on us - no trees for shade nor water to drink or bathe. For one person time not so tough on. Never been seen by those withering away on New Commoner's Island (Island of the beast). Metaphorically speaking, Island of the Beast still rings truth admittedly since within human nature we chain an internal beast. One rolling stone or better yet floating soul of bones can be shown via buzzing drones - meaning honeybees.

That's right far beyond the despondent desolation and leagues away from Shelly's company; Soundtrack lives atop the same old ship...more like a raft than ship. Beside a jetting rock in the middle of the deep blue sea you see bees swarming a rickety pile of wood. No kidding, ask Shelly and crew, all three were stung severely precluding a conference with Soundtrack, last week.

According to Preston's imagination the bees killed Soundtrack and fed the unfortunate man to the queen...horrific. Mina disagrees at this very moment, refuting Pretson's morbid supposition; Mina now with everything she's got, stands and rocks the boat holding rails to scream, "I know he's in there! He's alive I tell you he's alive, I can feel it!"

Shelly will not argue with a child's intuition, she places her eyes fixed on the bottom of a wishy - washy baseboard. Preston on the other hand doesn't want to face a swarm of angry bees and speaks his mind, "Okay Mina, what do you suggest we do?"

Mina's special, granted there's nothing worse on this planet than a bad person; yet there's nothing better than a good one and Mina has a good idea, "Take me within a hundred yards, I'll show ya."

Mina's already thinking cleverly by not explaining. She has saved her breath and the awesome ten year old with a mophead starts a breathing exercise. Shelly gets hit with sweet hope since she's seen Mina do this routine before. At peak of fishing in the Pond of Rosa, Mina became an expert diver.

Always sinking the net at deepest point then raising does the trick; as Mina would say back in heyday, "We catch best of the best by sinking our net!"

Preston rows at stern, Shelly focuses on synchronization as she watches Mina sitting in front of canoe. Shelly loves Mina. Mina loves Shelly but believe it or not, the child also has a crush on Soundtrack. Every breath inhaled by precious Mina recalls a time when she was drowning long ago. A storm swept through the islands, sweeping into the sea a small child about four or five years old. This child clung to an uprooted tree until pounding waves ripped the young one away from a natural float to go underwater for what felt similar to an eternity. Intrepid Mina kicked and swam with every muscle to surface but another wave would push her down to drown.

On the last endeavor to catch wind Mina wasn't saved by a whale, the sea didn't miraculously calm down but a man with a grip of one thousand reached into the water at just the right time! A miracle, the timing! Mina was reaching for air not a prayer. Soundtrack scooped up the child as a swooping bird does fish and best of all music was blaring. Mina spent every moment she had on deck staring into the eyes of a curious man. Soundtrack carried Mina back a hundred yards off shore of Common Island and tossed Mina into the water. Mina insisted (while treading), to stay aboard but the man shook his head and pointed to the island. She went underwater to swim back - Mina now recalls what she saw.

Preston has Mina snap out of her meditative state speaking directly after dropping paddle, "Okay, no more further, I see bees and hear buzzing."

Shelly stands tall, placing a flat hand over brow. She hopes to catch a glimpse of her friend but does not - been three months since Shelly stepped foot on Sountrack's big floppy deck. Shelly's not exactly worried more saddened by a new routine beginning, only Shelly would hop on board in the past but now Mina's gearing up for her sudden exclusivity. Mina pinches her nose and forces a puff of air through ear canals. Then, Mina yawns big time before taking a deep breath - the young girl dives in as a swimmer reacts to the gunshot. Courageous Mina swims underwater for roughly thirty yards and breaches similar to a whale hence to submerge again.

Shelly's too curious, she picks up her paddle and starts rowing to acquire a better view. Preston, instead of arguing places his head down and wraps both arms around his skull in hopes to not be stung. Mina didn't resurface. They saw Mina halfway take a breath and look around. Because Shelly loves Mina as a daughter - she jumps in the water.

Preston picks his head up noticing all the bees favor the leeward side of Soundtrack's float. Must be good timing, no bees on the attack ergo Preston hits Soundtrack's deck with his paddle calling out, "Hey cousin you in there?"

Nothing, only sound created by waves splashing against boats and a mild buzz - for the first circumstance this close to Soundtrack no music playing.

The past civilization had it so good the people made boomboxes and solar panels. Soundtrack was lucky enough to salvage what cassettes, compact discs he could. Sure Soundtrack's tracks are limited but better than nothing - perhaps even the captain grew tired of the sonic repetitiveness. Without having a rope to connect the boat to Soundtrack's, Preston keeps his cool and minds the canoe.

About thirty minutes go by till Preston harkens a new sound - laughter, awe. Preston smiles from ear to ear and feels great joy. The sun above saps Preston's easiness and just when he realizes his skin can't take anymore rays, Shelly and Mina simultaneously surface - along with a joyous burst of thankfulness for seeing their longtime friend. Preston of course has both arms out wide as if to tacitly say, "What is going on?" Mina and Shelly have no words to speak but plenty of giggles as they shimmy back onto the canoe.

Ready to leave, Soundtrack's door swings wide open and a thrown tarp emerges landing on trio's canoe. Happiness amongst all three brings out righteous hesitation. Rather than tearing at tossed gift, Mina, Preston and Shelly smile in direction of Soundtrack's boat. Unwrapping the blue tarp reveals some goods within. Expecting only a tarp for shield from the sun, Soundtrack was nice enough to pack in the middle an empty milk carton filled with fresh honey.

Nobody on the floating vessel has ever seen, tasted or smelled honey... so the nautical group of three are confused. Shelly thinks out loud, "Maybe patching for our hull?" Preston surmises otherwise, "Perhaps adhesive to attach tarp?" Mina though takes a long close-up look at this gold liquid inside an old translucent container and just then a bee alights on top - giving Mina an idea to lick the uncapped opening. Oh glory hallelujah!

Almighty does have mercy.

Mina's eyes light up. Her body stands on tip toes having Mina shout, "Thank you, thank you so much!" Preston and Shelly are bewildered but not being in the know doesn't last long - Mina hands Preston the jug, licking her fingers before and after hand-off. Mina's actions become contagious, Preston first, next Shelly - the taste of honey has them hop up and down like a funny bunny. Preston secures blue tarp around canoe, floating beside Soundtrack on a calm, sunny day.

The sun sets soon ergo Shelly suggests finishing tomorrow. An introduction to honey gives the three sweet dreams. Beneath a full moon, the canoe gently rocks side to side; stars twinkle in the night sky and all things swell till a crashing wave nearby awakes the sleeping triad. A breaching whale nudges the small canoe and its crew. All three grab hold of the sides in order to stay aboard. Luckily nobody panics. Instead they look at the luminescent water that shimmers bright blue then dissipates and disappears...what a show. Thinking what on Earth shines when water stirred has Mina, Shelly and Preston rock back to sleep until dawn.

The morning (as always), a sunny one. Shelly spots birds on the eastern horizon - these birds are traveling in the direction of old commoner's island, a place that initially harbored an endangered civilization now on the verge of extinction. Shelly recommends to her mates, "Let's set-up camp on old stomping grounds." Since the exodus (close to a year ago) nobody has stepped foot on the once crowded island and the idea spurs Preston ahead, picking up his oar, he turns boat for the east.

Mina starts her day with a finger full of honey to lick clean - creating back and forth bantor between Shelly and Mina about not using a licked finger to double dip. Mina concedes also agrees, her noggin bounces side to side during high tide on the ride. Easing their boat on old commoner's island; Mina's happy to see skittish wildlife, she orders Preston, "Stop! Don't row no more." Smart child, any more action would have surely caused a flock of wild geese to scatter. Mina points on shore and tells the crew, "Sea turtles!"

7

Best not to park on sand with animals around hence the group sits calmly before jumping off boat and into shallow water (ten feet off shore). After an hour of relaxing on the canoe, Mina's first to get into the water but not before Shelly utters, "Not so quick. You'll scare them away."

By them, Shelly means: a shoal, the salt-water geese, the gannets and gulls, ducks, turtles or even moles...oh cool also a lonesome iguana. Preston looks at Shelly with one desire in mind. He licks his lips staring at Shelly and declares, "I'm thirsty."

The day coming to an end, the sun sets certainly already on its way back. Tomorrow much like today and yesterday will bring about sunshine, glory but what good is the sun without fresh H_2O? Mina's buzzing from sugar while she spins in knee deep water. Preston with a defeated head down; prepares mind and body for death...it's been two days without water and the taste of honey has Preston crave a sip of nature's lifeline, make that a long swig.

Perhaps "The Fountain of Youth" simply pertains to fresh water, after all go days even less and people die but take a drink then we may carry on with more time, otherwise the expression would be "Fountain of Eternity." Preston doesn't look so good and Shelly has a feeling tomorrow will be his last if she does not acquire liquid. Shelly can't forestall nor hesitate. She has that sure-fire can-do attitude and tells Mina, "Stay here, we'll be back."

Resembling a lightning bolt without thunder, Shelly stands, grabs hold of oar and rows west using the North star as a compass. Where Shelly headed? No water on New Commoner's Island. Nothing other than a cesspool with desperate, dehydrating souls. A night of rowing gives Shelly a short nap until dawn and seems she had just the right idea, as geese fly overhead while she rises with a great yawn.

Preston awakes slumped over side rail of canoe. Then a group of gulls with ducks following show Preston where Shelly has taken them overnight...the gulls fly high above a mountain peak, a known mountain peak on scary Bantam Island.

Shelly knows Preston can't be witnessed in his weak condition or else Kingmon will feed the dieing man to those beastly bantams.

Preston asleep, Shelly splashes into shallow water and immediately met with large, black rocks. Sandy stretch of land around the largest boulder makes for an entrance; at the end Shelly meets a massive, iron door. No chance of breaking down this door, in fact the impenetrable impression has Shelly mesmerized. She wonders how did this come to be? Who made it and above all else...was construction done to keep out or trap in. Last time Shelly stepped foot here she had a bronze sword and her favorite pair of boots but those and that's neither here nor there.

Supposing Shelly bailed on current plan, what then? No water anywhere unless a storm approaches and not a cloud in sight has given Shelly Jibson an understandable fright...oh screw plight!

Remember hundreds of these ominous primates rule the trees. Years ago Shelly was picking a ripe mango when out of nowhere she nearly had herself torn limb from limb, literally. The Bantams, if need be, kill savagely by two pulling (in opposite directions) the victim's arms while two more do the same with your legs...horrendous. If that murderous action doesn't do the trick, then getting pounded out takes place...dreadful.

Anyway, Shelly (possessing courage and all) fluffs out to the right overgrown ivy covering a bell with a clapper. Shelly hesitates biting her bottom lip while perking eyebrows timidly. A deep breath and Shelly's ready to ring the bell but a coconut falls, not so fast. Fate had a different idea. Shelly's mouth expels a deep breath silently in relief. Still she misses her sword but a rock with a sharp edge will do. Around here that's no problem, pebbles compose the substrate alongside boulders with a jag. That milky jug of delicious juice bursts open the second it hit the rocky edge.

Wending on her way back to Preston, truthfully Shelly doesn't break stride as she opens the coconut (such action takes experience combined with familiarity) - you should've seen said move.

Swimming shortly with coconut held upwards, Shelly wakes up Preston while treading water, "Hey, got somethin' for you."

A few seconds go by and celebration swaps with worry. Preston's not getting up nor making a sound, oh no, not today. Suddenly the coconut becomes of no significance and tumbles out of her hand as she climbs aboard to eagerly investigate. Tarp thrown, body (by shoulders) lifted to face a worrisome woman who immediately pours tears while begging for Preston's consciousness to enliven.

Shelly (like a madman) hauls Preston off the boat. She becomes a lifeguard in the water then schleps his lifeless body advancing quickly to the iron door and Shelly doesn't shilly-shally, she rings the bell instantly upon arrival. No answer not even a holler or shake in the trees - Shelly rings again. Usually one round has Bantams scream as they jump limb to limb or the massive door (two feet thick) slides slowly open. Not this time. Shelly has stepped inside only once. The encounter created a tousle betwixt Kingmon and Shelly in which case Shelly stole Kingmon's ego after wearing the man out by avoiding every attack.

Fate brought Shelly here years ago. With vegetation and fruit trees, who in their right mind wouldn't check this place out? Well that was before Shelly knew what lived among the nature and prior to knowing an animalistic ape for a man loves beasts more than humans. Another instance took place last year and then Shelly refused a second unwelcome visit by staying in the boat - Mina, on the other hand, did not. Nevertheless, Kingmon meets with Preston regularly because they share a similar bloodline so on the third round of ringing the large bell – Shelly screams,

"Kingmon! Kingmon, open!"

Luck will have it, a bird in the tree spots Kingmon's expression of joy hearing Shelly's voice - almost a look as if he has missed her. Kingmon moves slowly to respond. The impenetrable entrance (one hundred yards away) will take a stroll down a path to answer. In the meantime, Shelly holds Preston's dangling body until she can no longer stand. After twenty minutes of treading easily along, Kingmon stops to pick a ripe fig when he hears a cry of agony, "Preston stay with me!" Only ten yards away Kingmon picks up his pace and opens this heavy door by removing a boulder wedged underneath - then drives his shoulder to budge the entrance open only enough to slip through onto sandy shore. For six years Kingmon has not seen the sea. The strong man was barely able to make it onto this shore (where he stands now) reminiscing on that day. Kingmon remembers how cold he was and most traumatically the way waves kept pounding against a head eager to breathe. Somehow or another Kingmon was tossed onto a large boulder and remained atop a black rock till dawn came. The storm subsided, the clouds scattered and water stopped pouring from above. Kingmon stood floundering at first but then saw a beautiful sight. The morning sun casted an ethereal glow among trees, a smell of flowers hit his unspoiled nose and from there he goes - jumping off the rock to swim on shore. First, Kingmon picked honeysuckle - delicious! Next he spotted a mango tree and after enjoying his maiden bite of fruit - Kingmon hollered loudly. Joy combined with satisfactory excitement, created a sonic wave reverberating throughout the small island - that's when Kingmon heard the Bantams' initial yowl. Starts with one long drawn out yelp enticing all to join at the beginning and when that unknown scream peaked so did Kingmon's fear. The grown man couldn't stop shaking from dread alone, the sounds moved closer towards a bald man afraid in the mango tree. Had there been one or two, perhaps even a pack Kingmon has the boldness to stand tall and fight if need be - but the sight of a hundred, each one with soulless eyes fixed upon; well a sight such as that can be intimidating.

One Bantam hops up to climb a flimsy branch, reaching out for Kingmon who snaps into fight mode and fends off a rabid looking creature. The slow nature and creepy stare never goes away. About three feet tall, hairy and muscular, these ominous primates group together making a pyramid of bodies. A Bantam ready to climb up stops at a howling sound on the outskirts. Each Bantam straightens as they disband. The Bantams' eyes no longer stare upwards at Kingmon nearly scared to death rather each has attention diverted - even Kingmon wonders what could be making a different howl. Kingmon watches these eerie animals track away as to find its source. Once Kingmon saw the coast was clear, he climbed down and decided that by whatever means necessary he wanted to win that creature's favor. In the very spot he stands now remembering a feeling to protect that which inhabits this fruitful island.

Kingmon witnesses Shelly Jibson tearfully begging for Preston to awake. Kingmon stands perplexed, after years living here he was able to not only befriend the Bantams but rule. How so? Kingmon fed the Bantams, with what? An unfortunate soul washed ashore one morning and Kingmon picked up a rock and bashed a fatigued man over the head. Then Kingmon let out the same enthusiastic yell while holding a dead body to feed on. The Bantams came and once they did, Kingmon tossed that beaten body over a pile of rocks. By standing tall and flashing his teeth he was able to stand his ground. Weeks went by and so did others on crappy floats. With tall trees and land being rare people were attracted as a moth is to a flame. Kingmon would nicely greet one or two, then attack from behind. Or he would deceive upwards having somebody look up in awe at delicious fruit only to whack the victim over the head. This went on as Kingmon patiently trained these small apes not to bite the hand that feeds. Kingmon's a doer not a thinker hence he quickly picks Preston up and throws a lifeless body over his shoulder. Moments ago Kingmon left door open and as Kingmon carries Preston with Shelly solemnly behind, a Bantam creeps out having eyes open wide. Never has this Bantam seen the ocean. Thick brush, high cliffs kept these... half chimp, half monstrous creatures satisfied with Bantam Island's forest until the day came when a man (Kingmon) decided to take fruit from the littoral trees and above all else - he screamed out loud as if to say, "My tree!"

Well, the minute Kingmon shimmied his scared tush down the mango tree, he started building. Big boulders all around this island except one spot where two giant (black) boulders have a five foot wide gap that leads into a forest area. This was where

Kingmon put whatever rock he could grab and carry to create a rock wall. When a Bantam climbed over, nearly destroying a make-shift barrier as it did so, Kingmon was always there with a woody spear ready to poke its eyes out at once. Kingmon put together a large fire on shore. Lived off the mango and nut trees around while he worked day into night - pounding rocks. Correct, pounding rocks, Kingmon carries a big rock up a hill in order to drop directly onto a bigger one below so the rocks break asunder. Why he did that was to get rest. At sundown the Bantams would become curious and one night Kingmon was tugged on the leg while sleeping and he luckily felt a stone beside him to throw. Next day sunlight shows Kingmon that the stone he threw was uncommon, mostly boulders take up all of Bantam Island.

That was then, this is now. A Bantam stares at the ocean - looks at Kingmon without a spear or stone then flashes its teeth. The Bantam shoved out by another one exiting fast and then another until all that's left of the Bantam population stares at the horizon over open ocean; each one with a look of awe - eyes and mouth open. A surreal scene changes, Kingmon holds Preston beside Shelly who stands still (frozen) waiting for courage to make the next step. The Bantams do the same, a stand still ensues momentarily. Nine, maybe ten small emaciated apes realize (at same time) this perhaps could be their final opportunity to survive. An amazed countenance changes as the whole group stares directly at Kingmon.

They first lick their lips, the Bantams sniff then lick air, suddenly advancing all at once.

Kingmon's bright idea - he throws Preston on sandy ground before him. The Bantam leader steps over lifeless Preston. Kingmon almost falls backtracking quickly away. Shelly then watches in horror as Kingmon trips over a rock and hits his head. In ankle deep water just on shore nine (maybe ten) Bantams stand and circle Kingmon only able to keep his head above water - he also has arms lifted in front of face as if to say, "Have mercy." Life's tough, no food about anymore. What's left to think about? One Bantam takes a left arm. One Bantam takes a right arm.

Oh my, two Bantams grab hold of each leg. Shelly knows what's about to happen; she bends her head down for this part. What Shelly does not see is the Bantam group stops right before ripping a wailing man apart.

Water swirls, a vortex near Kingmon's head, even a loosening of a deadly grip on Kingmon as something stirs beneath the oceanic surface - halting every Bantam's malicious act. Such a stunning moment of curiosity gives Kingmon the chance to crawl away. Stuck in a trance the scary group watches an eddy move closer and closer to their ankles. The screaming no longer present, Shelly looks up. Kingmon lies on his back gasping for air, while the Bantams stare and make way for what's swimming beneath. Air bubbles amaze the Bantams! More bubbles then the body becomes clear rising from the water to shake off like a beast - it's Mina!

Miraculous timing. You know that moment when your child matures by circumstance?

Here's an example; Shelly, Preston (out of it) and Kingmon stare at Mina freezing a once manic scene now made serene. The Bantams crouch beside Mina and each one has the same intention - to get the very best look at this unusual formation. Firstly, Mina possesses an attitude that walks the walk not having to talk. Secondly, her matted locks are unlike any human and important to mention - she's the same height.

The adult group of three instantly get a feeling Mina (here on out) can no longer be told what to do - why? She brought food. Mina has eyes locked on Preston who needs substance mostly. While advancing, Mina slings to her front side a net with many lobsters she has at her waist side. Before Preston and the others, Mina tosses a couple to circling Bantams still goggling at Mina in awe. Time to move on but no adult has a good idea on what to do with these eerie creatures standing near.

Preston needs water, so does Shelly and everybody back on Commoner's Island. On a small gap of sandy shore next to a cracked open iron door, Mina stands to retrieve dropped lobsters and shows these Bantams a food source. Mina picks two up (one in each hand).

She captures eye contact with one Bantam then rips the head off a lobster using her teeth. Afterwards carelessly drops the lobster at feet then spins for eye contact with another repeating the process. Monkey see, monkey do eat the lobsters but Mina's new pets didn't get the message; they don't have to spin and drop - they could just eat.

Mina stares and laughs; she soaks in her moment of circumstantial maturity. Shelly smiles dearly. She always knew Mina was something special. Oh life full of ups and downs, here we have happiness quickly drown by Mina's worried frown. Running as fast as her legs can carry, Mina slides into Preston like she just stole home. Preston's not waking up this time. Mina gets hit with a soulful and heavy feeling. She thinks it's her fault. Perhaps if she didn't soak in a moment of pride; Preston (her father figure) might still be alive. The Bantams come to Mina's side as she cries. There's no need to snap to. No root no food can bring Preston back - poor Preston didn't have water for three days. Mina feels Preston's lips with a finger tip, she's so sorry his lips are chapped and dry causing a flood of mature emotions to gush forth. Mina picks up her head to the sky and adding a most heart-wrenching cry she screams upwards, "No!" Over his dead body Mina whimpers. Shelly would join but she hasn't been rinsed in quite some time. Shelly stays lying on the ground not having the energy to move. Kingmon sits absorbing a heavy heart having to part. When one Bantam bites Preston's foot Mina screams, "No!" They instinctively react fast stopping at once.

Seems now the Bantams have a leader they will listen to. Kingmon picks himself up and walks over to Preston's body. Kingmon puts a hand on Mina's quivering shoulder. Mina smacks that hand off! Mina stands up. Mina's head stops at Kingmon's waist and yet this little girl's presence holds more weight. Mina shoves Kingmon breaking a grown man's stance. Before Kingmon speaks, Mina intterupts, "You didn't help! You could've helped years ago but always pushed him away!"

Mina shoves the man again. The pushing and shoving would have stopped there but Shelly was right, Kingmon's a snake.   15

Kingmon smacks Mina across the face causing a small child to hit the ground hard. For the first time since Mina walked on shore resembling a god, the Bantams stared intently but that changed instantly the second Mina was hurt. Nine could be ten of these three feet hairy, muscular animals stare intensely at Kingmon. Kingmon used to love these creatures but he sure doesn't love the look on their faces now - the monsters begin licking their lips.

One Bantam smells the air. Mina sits up and brushes a few locks aside as a beastly group advances towards Kingmon. Mina gives no order. She utters not a word to cease the first beast that ignites a live feast. Shelly covers her ears by use of hands to diminish the sounds of Kingmon's agony.

During the meal and now afterwards, Shelly went into a catatonic state. Recalling the time when she first heard those painful screams so penetrable. After an hour the Bantams have stripped Kingmon to the bone. Shelly sits woefully in total hopelessness. Mina on the other hand has begun digging a grave for Preston. As would a canine or turtle on steroids, Mina digs vigorously into the sandy soil. Only she has no intention on building a sandcastle rather a resting place for Preston. The Bantams do what Mina has been doing for an hour till she no longer must dig; four or five finish the job - Mina stands to state, "No, deep enough." These animalistic helpers stop at once.

Mina slowly walks to Preston's corpse when struggling with a heavy and limp load Shelly helps out - Mina didn't even see her approach. From there the two carry a dear friend not only to his grave but their hearts forever - amen.

Confusion sets in, the primal creatures around Mina and Shelly become curious. Drawn in by the humans' mood, the animals creep closer to Mina and Shelly standing sweetly at Preston's filled grave. Mina takes out a blue flower she had twisted in her thickest lock and gently tosses onto ground. Mina cries heavily. Shelly's had enough pain, she looks upwards.

A hairy appendage comes into play - a Bantam grabs Mina's hand. Every Bantam stares at Mina and begins to feel something stirring inside. One action separates humans from animals - crying. The sight of this has Bantams feel a sentiment hence a reason for a new sound, one to cover and smother life's anguish. Wild animals adapt all sorts of sounds in substitute tears. These Bantams here come from a place once called Indonesia but the flood (a few hundred years ago) washed them away - taking salvation on a buoyant coconut tree. One item was with those hairy creatures as Mother Nature's float drifted - a bongo.

Months went by and some Bantams dried then died. When a body started to rot the Bantams hurled a cadaver into the sea; the first time a Bantam drummed the bongo afterwards to drown out an agonizing cry before one died. So its only right the drums presently start. A Bantam breaks away - briskly comes back to join the beat. Seems they all stashed a drum buried in the dirt just a jog away. A sad group perks up at a rhythmic beat now made by small creatures. One hollers at a moment, repeating the process to create a vocal rhapsody. Shelly's mind and body changes from suffocation to light peace.

Mina hears thunder. Shelly hears thunder. Clouds coalesce above creating an instant downpour of what? What? - Water! The Almighty's gift for good behavior. Rain showers Bantam Island. Miraculously water flows from cliffs above making a fresh water pool. Steep cliffs trickle water at first, after an hour that stream waxes a waterfall. At ground level a pond rises and channels towards Preston's grave. Mina snaps into action and starts digging again creating a channel to divert water away from grave site. Bantams follow the leader and many hands make light work. Quickly dug canals moved water in proper directions that now create a moat surrounding Preston's grave.

For hours water pours making a strong brook that gushes through Kingmon's iron door. Shelly and Mina take apart rock wall Kingmon built by smelting rocks with help from a volcanic vent. They place rock fragments alongside make-shift gullies for improvement. Shelly operates as a workhorse until her legs and arms give out. Exhaustion takes over Shelly Jibson's body- she naps nearby. The rain lets up helping Mina build a tee-pee for a mother figure. Anything Mina does the Bantams follow suit getting the hang of any task their tenacious leader begins. Throughout the night shelter was made just for Shelly and when this rested woman arises she's greeted with piles of prizes. Shelly throws open vegetative door and strewn on ground beholds: figs, peaches, almonds, herbs, mangos and bananas.

Shelly's initial thought...she misses Preston, he too would love this present day smorgasbord.

As Shelly explores close terrain, she chooses a handful of figs to accompany her on a stroll. Coming across Kingmon's skeleton, Shelly notices the Bantams stopped at the ankles, leaving behind big brown boots. Taking a look around unveils absence of everyone. Mina's gone somewhere, the Bantams are not in sight. Shelly can't resist her urge - she takes Kingmon's big brown boots for herself. Shelly's only thought now...where on Earth is that prodigious child?

Over night Mina took the canoe to Commoner's Island (miles away). One Bantam went with Mina - the canoe reaches Commoner's Island. At first glance, seems no life exists. Mina hops out, Bantam stays behind awing down at fish below water surface. Not much to look at around here anymore, flys buzz but nobody else does because the people who took over the landscape did nothing other than consume and contaminate. What a shame. Mina takes in a moment where her favorite coconut tree used to be. Nothing but a stump now. A plentiful tree chopped down, burned and destroyed. Mina remembers climbing to the top when she was younger.

Everyone clamored below for a sweet throw. Since no one is present...Mina starts crying.

An ulterior shout close by has Mina snap out of momentary sadness. Arriving at the once Pond of Rosa, now turned puddle of mud, Tim and Jim are on hands and knees. Mina runs (coming in hot) to question Tim and Jim,

"Are you okay? I brought a coconut here."

Jim stops task, Tim stops task. Both men freeze on hands and knees while no longer feeling the impulse to pinch so to consume muddy substance. The coconut halts these two dire looking men. Jim erupts from excitement. Tim simmers the exuberance by "shushing" his sidekick.

Mina again offering, "Here, take it."

Tim stares deeply at Mina as does Jim. Before accepting Tim says two words in the most grateful tone, "Thank you."

Mina must know avaunt another question up at Tim with Jim, "Where's everybody else?"

Ripping the coconut's outer flesh happily Tim replies, "All dead." Mina can't believe it, "Everybody?"

Tim with Jim take turns at giving that coconut all they got and become quiet - Mina gets an uneasy feeling.

The way these men look now scares Mina. As she backs up, their faces can barely be seen anent the fact mud covers everything but their eyes. Always filled with good ideas, she now has a bad idea about what may have transpired here. An opportunity to leave makes Mina turn away - that coconut might be the only diversion around and Mina doesn't want to be here when they get done tearing it apart. Mina (eager to part) walks back to the canoe driven ashore. She returns with her head down imagining horrific events in the past. Mina looks up (now on sand).

A young boy stands eerily still staring at the Bantam on the canoe. Even the Bantam seems frightened by a young boy who slowly turns his skull knowing Mina's there without looking. The boy holds a bronze sword that glimmers in rays of sun asking profoundly,

"Where's my father, what have you done?"

Show down...Mina freezes and does nothing - sometimes the wisest course of action. The child remains glaring into the eyes of an uneasy primate. Mina's eyebrows shift up casting wonderful gaze at inquisitive kid. After a minute of silent tension, the four feet tall menace speaks up this time spitting on the ground below prior utterance,

"Where's my father?"

With a sense of humor Mina wonders, "Who your daddy?"

Not funny, not today anyway because the angry boy stomps fastly towards Mina's wide stance. Shelly back in the day taught Mina a tactic of combative avasion that takes place right now. As quick as the dirty boy moves - Mina's faster. When he lunges Mina darts to the left or right and she appears to have been born in a sandbox judging based on animalistic use of her arms to make up for another set of legs.

The boy too slow to grab hold of Mina - perhaps rage makes the boy think if he grapples Mina he may be able to wring the truth out of her lungs. Catching wind with hands on knees the enraged boy huffs and puffs looking directly at Mina smiling. He was angry before but now with that smug look on her face he wants Mina dead. Anger creates tension, rage makes wrath. Anger has us think of picking up a rock, wrath makes you do it without thought - so the boy sees a big rock at his feet. Without hesitation a small and furious child begins an act of intentional murder, when a booming vocal sound stops the murderous throw, "Hey, what you doin' boy?"

Only proper to match intensity hence Tim standing fifty yards away picks up his rock and hollers while advancing,

"I'll tag you back Dick Jr!"

An intense man ready to pounce at a boy ready for war creates peace, strangely. Instincts have Dick Junior subside. Mina stunned by what she felt. A tussle sure, maybe even a slap but what she saw in that boy just a moment ago scares Mina back to the canoe without breaking her stare. As fast as she can paddle Mina leaves a once beautiful piece of land now reduced to sin.

With the sun setting after a mishap Mina loses her bearings. She stands in canoe fifty yards off shore. Sadly she should've done that an hour ago because the sun always led the way to Bantam Island by a crepuscular shadow which cannot be seen now - oh no on top of uneasiness a storm approaches suddenly. Waves pick up. Thunder cracks. Lightning strikes above. You'd think Mina panics or becomes scared, well then you don't know Mina! She was born in these conditions almost as if Mina evidently enjoys the rocking of a boat and spraying from water all around.

What's the worst that could happen? Oh she could be tossed into the sea and never seen again - good Mina experienced that time ago and met her first crush. One thing has Mina perturbed and that's the sight of a sweet monkey obviously scared in front. She's got beauty, strength and wit. What good are those attributes without sensitivity. Mina showcases the greatest characteristic; she flounders moving to front of canoe.

A sweet and lost child grabs the creature's hand assuring over sounds of thunder,

"Don't worry. Hang on!"

Nighttime was rough. Morning breaks and shows Mina no land in sight. No stars out last night. Mina has no idea on Earth where Bantam Island peaks over this vast blue sea. A small canoe holding the life of Mina and her pet begins to show decrepitude. A leak at the base begins flooding a canoe that soon will not be a vessel. Mina must act fast, thought before paddling has a hasty girl remember what Shelly said years ago, "Always follow the sun."

Well Shelly Jibson your wise maxims are of no use today! Not with the radiant star straight up. Mina smacks her bottom lip with a dry tongue. She takes a guess and heads for land, any land.

As the sun sets Mina and her monkey friend are sure to keep the gold star in front rather than behind them. Dusk arrives and Mina can no longer row - her company couldn't take part helping given the fact only one paddle came with canoe. Mina's worst enemy creeps onto her senses as snares on bears - thirst. Sweet child of ours can not swallow. Her throat and mouth too dry - soon, without water Mina will die.

People spoke back in the day about spring water. Thirst makes Mina remember vividly, almost like the words were uttered yesterday,

"Did you hear? Did you hear? Water's here!"

Goodness gracious Mina smacks an even dryer tongue across lips chapping.

Looking up hopefully, Mina does next what could be the life or death of aqua-girl. She jumps in.

Treading water she beseeches a timid ape that goes back and forth from making a decision.

"Come. Come," Mina says above the surface of warm sea-water. Finally, monkey see, monkey do jump in ocean - about time because the old float no longer holds water or a title of any kind other than rotten log. Immediately Mina begs and informs her mate,

"Don't drink!"

The animal doesn't speak a word of English but gets the point.

Mina first ahead, monkey follows the leading girl. After a minute Mina gets a bad feeling in the middle of her swim stroke. Mina looks back as a mama duck for her assurance. Problem, big problem, monkey gone - monkey can't swim. Oh the remorse! She didn't make sure or even doubt that her friend could swim. Clever girl, she darts underwater spotting a lifeless creature five feet below surface.

With friend held tight in arms, Mina emerges - barely catching wind. Here we have humanity at its finest. Albeit a scenario most difficult nevertheless one that demonstrates a holy spirit - Mina kicks and doggy paddles for two lives. If she goes down well then so be it, she'll die trying. Sun completely tucked away. Stars are coming out. Hard to watch an innocent child subjected to such misfortune, even more so because Mina's a good person.

If this current girl was given some sort of lifeline or lifesaver, who knows what kind of woman she would become. Times like these are tough to bear witness to. Much tougher for the soul having to bear. Mina can hardly take a breath. Her exhaustion and dear friend are weighing her down - before sinking Mina expels a sound, "No!"
My goodness...she even kicks and swims underwater. Youth meets an unknown feeling - depletion. Prior to muscles shutting down (beneath water), Mina puts out one last spasm of a swim stroke. She goes limp and sinks like a stone. Brown skin, brown eyed girl named Mina with mocha matted hair gave it all she had but Mother Nature made a defeatable human not a machine.

Sweet child of ours uses last move to hold hands with the Bantam - same one which shared a bond during Preston's burial. So happens the sinking ape has one last move also - that is to affirm grip. If not energy only a single power can save Mina from the dark depth. Luckily for the limp child she has earned her soul power; a grey bottle-nose dolphin (out of the blue) rushes to scoop up the pair with finesse and style - quickly hitting the surface. When the dolphin breeches (with Mina holding tight to monkey friend) it explodes a gush of breath (from blowhole) that knocks the wind not out but back in duo. As Mina takes in much needed air, so does the small ape. The blowhole came along with an explosion of air so powerful both Mina and monkey grab dorsel fin; while expressing a countenance similar to a boxer retrieving a heavy blow.

Now riding on the back of a dolphin, Mina's in no mood to be excited until the sun shines on her face and another dolphin (to the side) catapults out of water performing a quadruple back flip. Following another - its a whole, holy pod. Each spinning, flipping dolphin out does one another to buoy Mina's spirits.
After a hundred yards of towing Mina, while every dolphin springs from the ocean; the scene catches attention of a man who could use some action today - Soundtrack.

No sails on Soundtrack's raft just a rickety baseboard with a center hut. The dolphin carries Mina to Bantam Island. About a league from Bantam Island Soundtrack begins paddling as always with a dispassionate attitude until a flock of geese fly over - heading toward Bantam Island. So Soundtrack (a weathered man) picks up his pace, then a flock of blue ducks fly overhead low enough nearly skimming the top of Soundtrack's bald head.
Now Soundtrack gets really excited and if it wasn't for the awesome cargo he possesses on board he'd jump in because the man can swim.
 Those blue ducks land on water, using their belly with feet for an aquatic meet and greet.

The noisy geese alight on Bantam's Island sandy patch that has a curious Shelly Jibson wonder, what on earth afoot? Running like a child, Shelly dodges natural obstacles on Bantam Island's terrain. Shelly's kind of tall and not built for eager sprinting, consequently Shelly trips and falls hard. A hardened individual with shoulder length sorrel hair shakes off an injury that encroaches onto a mind for the rest of her trip (to the sandy opening where animals are making a ruckus). Now limping and approaching shore, Shelly's mind knows what just happened. She twisted her knee badly. Shelly falls onto sand after debushing. She may not be able to stand but Shelly sees a spectacle as lead dolphin rushes into shallow waters - stopping on sandbank at ankle deep water as a jet ski would. Mina far too exhausted to do anything other than breathe.

The Bantam Mina has with her begins to pet Mina while whimpering. Not a human and obviously now not a monster either because the Bantam shows emotion.

Grabbing hold of Mina schlepped over the dolphin's back-side, the bantam looks up and expels a most heart-wrenching howl. A howl that reverberates for miles, suddenly what's left of the Bantam's population emerges from woodlands. Nine possibly ten small creatures help carry Mina off a dolphin that needs movement.

A powerful scene last night gave these wild animals a special feeling; seems they know just what to do. One Bantam takes a leg and another the other leg. Same with Mina's arms, they do this before ripping a threat or person to five pieces. Shelly on hands and knees looks on in horror; she thinks The Bantams are putting Mina out of her misery. So with all the gas she has left within her bodily tank,
Shelly screams aloud, "No!"
Not even a head turns to look. The Bantams are adjusting Mina as each one supports a little girl's depleted body. As the animalistic group passes a broken woman lying down on sandy shore, Shelly reaches a hand out in Mina's direction. Worried about future incident Shelly (barely able to move) yells, "What are you doin' with her?"

The group walks through Bantam Island's path arriving at burial site where land has been cleared. The storm last night brought rain whereupon the sun's rays soaked up almost all liquid. The waterfall nearby no longer has water. Gullies with rocky buffers do not have running water. Even the land has lost moisture but one spot still miraculously holds water. The moat that Mina dug with Bantams was made for the purpose of keeping water away from Preston's gravesite. Mina had a feeling so strong when the time came to divert the water she dug deep enough creating a lifeline. A trench about three feet wide and six feet deep encircles Preston's grave.

A few Bantams adjust Mina one last time in arms then hurl her lifeless body into holy moat. No kicking or swimming. All bantams stare downwards at a little girl who sinks out of sight beneath beneath dark water.
Bubbles. More bubbles break the surface. A matter of seconds has Mina return to surface. Along with the exuberant child an explosion of happy emotion emerges from moat. Mina's in no rush to get out. She gulps in water while playfully swimming.

Oh sweet Shelly, so worrisome of what's happening to a dear child disrupts Mina's brief period of happiness by screaming down the path (crawling on hands and knees) - again Shelly whoops,

"Mina, Mina!" Mina hops out of moat quickly attempting to ease Shelly's worry. Meeting Shelly halfway down the path, Mina comes to Shelly's aid, "Shelly you okay?"

Shelly's so happy. Looking up at Mina she has no words only watery eyes and a big smile. Mina and Shelly have a moment until they spot a figure at the end of pathway (down toward shoreline). A person or something stands eerily staring at Mina (on ground) with arms wrapped around Shelly. Mina curious and brave enough to investigate does so. Walking slowly the small drenched, rejuvenated child seems frightened by what she comes across at end of trail. At first it was a shadow. On approach the shadow took shape - Soundtrack standing still looking into Shelly's eyes not Mina's. Mina tugs at Soundtrack's crispy shorts made of linen. Whether it be a broken heart or curious mind, Mina angrily speaks to Soundtrack, "Hey down here! what's wrong with you?" Soundtrack looks as if he has seen a ghost. Shelly takes in scenario wondering also, "What's up? Why you lookin' at me like that?"

Soundtrack backs up. Mina moves with Soundtrack and tugs once again on shorts so ragged. This time Mina pulls a piece of fabric off. Mina very confused starts tearing up as Soundtrack continues to back away. A silent and stunned man gets back onto his small float. Mina knows better than to swim and climb on deck. She hollers off Bantam's sandy shore, "What's wrong?"

Close enough to hear a reply Mina harkens a reason for Soundtrack's departure,

"Cursed defeat come to those with boots on the feet."

Mina has known Soundtrack her entire life and never has she witnessed nor felt such emotion from a usually nice man. Soundtrack saw Shelly down the path in a small amount of distress and what did he do? He just stood there frozen as if petrified so now Mina ponders while watching a person she loves paddle away into the horizon nearing twilight hour. He didn't even say goodbye.

Mina too frozen by a jilted sentiment stands there wondering till Shelly screams out horrifically, "Stop!"

A sound gushing from the heart and gut of Shelly makes Mina run like the good old days - sprinting to Shelly's succor. Mina makes record time through trail. Hurdling over a boulder, similar to a track star, Mina's at Shelly's side in a moment's notice. Shelly's not crying or pouting, only happy to see Mina and that she isn't alone because those Bantams scattered the second Mina approached at lightning speed. Shelly's happiness covered up the fact one nasty Bantam took a chunk out of Shelly's calf muscle. Perhaps Shelly Jibson's in shock (what a gift) because she stares at Mina without a care in the world, when a little girl espies the most graphic wound. A gash so deep, Shelly's muscle tissue has become exposed. Shelly doesn't look down at injury only keeps staring at Mina who suddenly becomes a nurse. Mina rips off the one shirt she has to wrap Shelly's leg tight and the second she finishes - Mina scans the Bantam group with furious eyes and clinched fists. Going down the line as general to soldiers; Mina sees what she's looking for - blood on lips. Mina's anger begins to boil, face to face with guilty Bantam. Mina, the same height matches Bantam's physique appearing for a short while that a battle will break out any second. The remaining group disbands no longer standing side by side. They all stand beside Mina. Not a showy feeling of guilt from solo Bantam. After a deep breath Mina calms down but points with order for that Bantam to go elsewhere. Good choice of action because the mean Bantam backs away like a creep would - not turning around rather walking backwards with a soulless stare.

Mina becomes aware that now she will have something to worry about on the outskirts. Shelly sweetly crawls to Mina's feet. Oh my, quickly Mina changes her attitude from still soldier to concerned mother. Quite a show of stupendous spirit from a child.

Meanwhile Soundtrack, a bald man having a grey thick beard arrives at his destination - Commoner's Island. Whereabout expecting such desolation seems to be in good spirits. Soundtrack's a grown man who took up the lifestyle of living on a boat decades ago. Since his boat will soon not float, Soundtrack looks around then loses hope. Not a tree, shrub or bush in sight. Not even a plant.

Soundtrack places a flat hand on forehead expressing an attitude of good grief. When a figure appears (up on a hill) to the west, Soundtrack spots life. The hand placed on forehead now flipped over to block a setting sun. Soundtrack in awe freezes the same way as before only this time, Soundtrack relishes what he sees; a small boy with a sword looms on a hill.

Wrapped tightly around neck, Dick Junior has a black cobra with its head and tongue peaking over the boy. The bald and bold man approaches for a better look then Dick Junior takes a juicy bite out of an apple.

Alright...so a friendly woman in distress Soundtrack repels from, meaning back on Bantam Island with Shelly. But an unfamiliar boy adjoined and seemingly also possessed with a black cobra catches this stunned man's attention.

Soundtrack walks up a mound. Dick Junior takes another bite juicier than the last. Apple juice trickles down the chin of a boy who makes no attempt to welcome. Soundtrack gestures first (halfway up the mound) by lifting a hand combining language,

"Hey there boy."

Instead of a gesture, Junior takes another bite and finishes the green apple. After tossing apple to the side Dick Junior rubs juice on forearms, then licks his lips as does the cobra around neck and head area. Soundtrack stops short of hilltop. He speaks again, "Hope you got one for me." Now kind of frustrated, Soundtrack steps closer with authority thinking about his own seniority to say,

"Don't you be disrespecting me boy, you the only one around here?"

Since no reply has been made from Junior atop a grassy knoll, Soundtrack goes as close as anybody would given three facts: One this rude boy has a mean looking cobra ready to strike, two...Junior has a formidable sword and finally for Soundtrack's sound train of thought - they don't know each other. Soundtrack turns to walk away. After all if the manly stranger kept grilling a little chit, who's the rude person then? Aggression was not useful. So Soundtrack (nearly at bottom of hill) shouts aloud,

"I don't know what I'm gonna do with all my goods."

Soundtrack stops, turns back around and yells up that hill to an impolite tyke you want to smite,

"Hey, you speak language or just some jerk?"

Nothing else to do, Soundtrack drops his guard and ego as he approaches intense Dick Junior who now eats a banana! Soundtrack must know so here he goes marching up the mound. Slowly he beseeches, "Where on earth you gettin' that goody good good?"

Soundtrack's tone lightened. His voice softened thus a man's demeanor changed to submission garnering Dick Junior's attention. Junior speaks profoundly, "Whatever you please."

Well, that's not really a full thought but Soundtrack sure is happy to hear from this scary boy. Soundtrack keeps at it verbally,

"I don't see any trees about."

Soundtrack's correct. Without vegetation and open terrain an amateur explorer could say this island doesn't harbor life. Boy explains calmly after a few breaths, "Really want to know?"

Feeling a connection, Soundtrack tracks further up the hill when Dick Junior interrupts the man's answer to a rhetorical question,

"I'll show you."

The closer Soundtrack becomes, the more tense the black cobra seems to be thus a curious man keeps his distance and stays a few feet away just in case.

The sun straight up, nothing around but these two and a snake - Dick Junior takes his eyes off Soundtrack. About four feet tall, wearing a cobra at the neck and old foliage around waist area Dick Junior shows how on Earth he eats delicious fruit. The child speaks while staring into the sun, "Must picture your desire." Then the kid opens his mouth wide as if appearing to swallow solar rays . The black cobra does the exact action simultaneously. A green apple plops and drops from the cobra's mouth onto Junior's hand without a nervous flinch to catch. The child gently pitches apple to Soundtrack who is too stunned to eat right away. Seconds of standing still ensues till Soundtrack has a bite. Unlike any apple before this one (spat out by a venomous snake) bears more juice and zest than the rest. What Soundtrack doesn't know while he swallows last bit, that apple came with a silent stipulation.

The boy has a burning question at once,
 "Have you seen my father?"
Confused and satisfied Soundtrack replies immediately,
 "I'm sorry, what?"
Dick Junior reverts to original demeanor that starts with two furious eyeballs on a man that was given a life saving piece of fruit. Junior and his cobra face Soundtrack. The child moves one step towards the man who begins to feel dread. Again Junior asks,
 "My father, where's my father?"
Soundtrack has a sense of humor. He eggs the boy on vocally,
 "Guess your cobra can't spit out that, huh?"
Before Soundtrack could laugh the cobra strikes a great bald man with a grey beard directly on the face. The cobra's mouth hit at his eyebrow down to the bottom lip area of a friendly man who will most certainly be missed by a little girl.

As Soundtrack retrieves sudden strike, he looks down at an apple in his hand that's rotten to the core. Soundtrack falls on his knees as venom courses through his blood causing immense pain. Soundtrack murmurs under bated breath, "No."
Dick Junior does a 360 degree spin that ends with Soundtrack's decapitation.

Dick Jr. regresses back to usual attitude of stillness lacking emotion. Soundtrack lies split in two atop hill. Dick Junior becomes sinister looking because the unwholesome boy can't take his eyes off the blood on the bronze blade. If that action wasn't creepy enough, licking his lips outdoes.
The world has some sort of natural, relentless and infinite balance. For example, here's a lost boy atop a natural hill just when Tim alongside Jim has relentless Dick Junior snap out of what could have been an infinite feeling. Surprise does the trick with a burst of language. Tim (a tall, slender bloke) calls out loud to a morbid boy,
 "That's the third one I've seen. Keep it up tiger."
Survival, Soundtrack (a strange person to Tim and Jim) is dead. Why fuss?
Tim doesn't have a cobra. Jim has no sword - and the stranger is decapitated so Jim has something to say. He stutters before communicating, "t.t.t. to the boat."

The idea and sentence did not make sense. Such excitement with fear brought out an instinct to speak. The intensity made Jim stutter and he couldn't put together a coherent idea or sentence, thus a mind summoned an old sentence. Tim pauses.

Dick Junior still atop grassy knoll lording over Soundtracks body. Jim has an idea but can't muster up the words. Tim looks onto Jim with wonder because the man didn't always stutter. Jim (a small adult) uses more body language now. He jumps up and down pointing at Soundtrack's corpse. Jim then points in direction of shore where Soundtrack came from. Tim knows Jim well and since Jim suddenly picked up a speech impediment, Tim informs Dick Junior, "Oh, he's saying let's go see if he has any goods."
Boy, did that get Junior's attention. Walking over Soundtrack's torso Dick Junior advances to the tactful pair with a good idea.

Too close for comfort, Tim and Jim are sure to keep a safe distance between them. Jim has the personality of a loyal dog off its leash who leads the way and looks back repeatedly until all three arrive on the west side of this uninhabitable island where Soundtrack drove his decrepit float ashore. Tim and Jim must move quickly. In a moment what's left of a raft that was once a home will be gone. Hauling the heavy timber onto dry land becomes an impossible task given the facts, Tim and Jim are malnourished. The heavy timber weighs twice as much originally because the wood has absorbed sea-water. Like two cat-burglars Tim and Jim hop onto a float that breaks apart as they ransack a dead man's old home.

Everything except a jug of honey made the trip. Not much left, Tim does the hopeful tilt of container to view what's left inside. Jim begins stuttering from the excitement. Jim has been around long enough to have been told by folklore what honey is and where the sweet nectar comes from but he can't spit out the words. He hops up and down while pointing at the jug held high in Tim's right hand. This action has Tim look at Jim in a new way, unlike any expression put forth on Tim's face.

When Tim's eyes begin to water from fondness towards his sidekick's happiness; he stares at Jim jumping for joy when that malicious boy pierces Jim's stomach with a sharp toy. From heaven to hell, Tim's face tells the story. Tim's jaw drops and eyes pop as Jim stops hopping. He's hunched over, holding his stomach and now Jim can hardly stand. Tim can't believe what unjustly happened. He drops honey container without a care to catch his friend before he hits the ground. With a final breath and eyes locked onto a dear friend who has arms wrapped around him sweetly; Jim doesn't stutter or stammer, finishing his life in a righteous manner, Tim hears and feels a man's last words,

"I love you brotha'."

After death, Tim gazes into the eyes of a greedy boy who ate all the honey. Tim stands up to express,

"You shouldn't have done that."

Dick Junior has no qualms on talking,

"Where's my father?"

Tim doesn't answer and he will not answer since his brother lies slain at his feet. Tim backs away. Keeping his eyes fixed on a sadistic boy, Tim disappears around the hill.

Dick Junior motivated by natural means doesn't think twice. He begins swimming. Growing up on a now forsaken island, Dick Junior witnessed and felt his father's urge to thrive elsewhere. Everybody failed to make it. Dick Junior has a relentless attitude. He swims all day and through the night (with a black cobra aside) until twenty four hours later, Junior spots a landmass peaking out of the infinite water. A large mountain, big black boulders and lush trees has Dick Junior become hasty and a hundred yards off shore he fumbles his sword underwater. Junior has a natural instinct not to swim beneath the surface so he continues toward land. Destiny has an exhausted boy crawl on sand exiting shallow water when he's met with a pretty sweet sight.

Mina stands tall looking directly at Dick Junior who absorbs the scenery. Junior sees pubescent Mina without her blouse and she has her lips covered in honey. Junior forgets intentions and realizes he can't communicate because now he has a stutter.

www.ingramcontent.com/pod-product-compliance
Lightning Source LLC
Chambersburg PA
CBHW020322150626
46552CB00022B/3155